W9-CFB-642
ASCAP
MELE KALIKIMAKA
Words and Music by
R. ALEX. ANDERSON
Brightly (not too slowly)
Jin — gle Bells up-on a steel gui — tar
mp
Through the palms we see the same bright star
Chorus
Me — le Ka — li — ki — ma — ka is the thing to say On a
mf
bright Ha — wai — ian Christ — mas day
That's the is — land greet. — ing that we send to you From the
land where palm trees sway
Here we know that Christ — mas will be green and bright The
sun to shine by day and all the stars that night
Me — le Ka — li — ki — ma — ka is Ha — wa — ii's way to
say Mer — ry Christ — mas to you
1
2
you
(c) Copyright 1949, 1950 by MCA MUSIC, A Division of MCA, INC., New York, N. Y. Sole Selling Agent MCA MUSIC, A Division of MCA, Inc., 445 Park Ave., New York, N. Y. 10022. Used by Permission. All Rights Reserved.

KE AHIAHI MAMUA O KALĪKIMAKA

'Twas the Night before Christmas

–in Hawai'i–

illustrated by
Barbara Ewald

creative concept by
MeneHune

translations-pronunciations by
Lynette 'A'alaonaona Roy

graphic design by
Richard Priest, Suzanne Kittrell, William Kealy, Lisa Andes

edited by
Valjeanne Budar

based on the original poem by
Clement C. Moore

"Mele Kalikimaka" by
R. Alex Anderson

THE BESS PRESS
3565 Harding Ave. Honolulu, Hawai'i 96816
(808) 734-7159 www.besspress.com

Pronunciation Guide

Most of the vowel sounds in the Hawaiian language are uniform and consistent. *A* has the sound of *ah*. *E* has the short sound of *e* as in *lend*. *I* has the long sound of *ee* as in *feet*. O has the long sound of *o* as in *old*. *U* has the sound of *oo* as in food.

Hawaiian is a fluid and melodious language that is very gentle and smooth to the ears. The vowels are often run together for better and easier pronunciation.

The use of the glottal stop (') frequently distinguishes Hawaiian from other Pacific languages. Where noted, a glottal stop indicates a short, abrupt pause in speech.

The Hawaiian language also uses a semi-V sound (as in the word *lawa*), which employs a combinaton of the V and W, creating a smooth suggestion of the V.

Stress or accent in Hawaiian pronunciation is usually placed on the next-to-last syllable and alternating preceding syllables. Five-syllable words, however, have accentuated first and fourth syllables. Another exception to the basic rule occurs when a macron (¯) is shown above a vowel within a syllable (i.e., kanakē), which is then treated with the greatest stress.

ISBN: 1–880188–92–9
Library of Congress Catalog Card Number: 94-77954
Printed in Hong Kong

dedicated to
our greatest
gifts of all—
our children

'Twas the night before Christmas, when all through the house
Not a creature was stirring, not even a mouse;
The stockings were hung by the chimney with care,
In hopes that St. Nicholas soon would be there;
The children were nestled all snug in their beds,
While visions of sugar-plums danced in their heads;
And Mamma in her 'kerchief, and I in my cap,
Had just settled our brains for a long winter's nap;
When out on the lawn there arose such a clatter,
I sprang from the bed to see what what was the matter.
Away to the winaow I flew like a flash,
Tore open the shutters and threw up the sash.
The moon, on the breast of the new-fallen snow,
Gave the lustre of mid-day to objects below,
When, what to my wondering eyes should appear,
But a miniature sleigh, and eight tiny rein-deer,
With a little old driver, so lively and quick,
I knew in a moment it must be St. Nick.
More rapid than eagles his coursers they came,
And he whistled, and shouted, and called them by name;
"Now, Dasher! now, Dancer! now, Prancer and Vixen!
On, Comet! on, Cupid! on, Donder and Blitzen!
To the top of the porch! to the top of the wall!
Now dash away! dash away! dash away all!"
As dry leaves that before the wild hurricane fly,
When they meet with an obstacle, mount to the sky;
So up to the house-top the coursers they flew,
With the sleigh full of Toys, and St. Nicholas too.
And then, in a twinkling, I heard on the roof
The prancing and pawing of each little hoof—
As I drew in my head, and was turning around,

Down the chimney St. Nicholas came with a bound.
He was dressed all in fur, from his head to his foot,
And his clothes were all tarnished with ashes and soot;
A bundle of Toys he had flung on his back,
And he look'd like a pedlar just opening his pack.
His eyes—how they twinkled! his dimples how merry!
His cheeks were like roses, his nose like a cherry!
His droll little mouth was drawn up like a bow
And the beard of his chin was as white as the snow;
The stump of a pipe he held tight in his teeth,
And the smoke it encircled his head like a wreath;
He had a broad face and a little round belly
That shook, when he laughed, like a bowl full of jelly.
He was chubby and plump, a right jolly old elf,
And I laughed, when I saw him, in spite of myself;
A wink of his eye and a twist of his head,
Soon gave me to know I had nothing to dread;
He spoke not a word, but went straight to his work,
And fill'd all the stockings; then turned with a jerk,
And laying his finger aside of his nose,
And giving a nod, up the chimney he rose;
He sprang to his sleigh, to his team gave a whistle,
And away they all flew like the down of a thistle.
But I heard him exclaim, ere he drove out of sight,
"Happy Christmas to all, and to all a good night."

Clement C. Moore,
1862, March 13th. originally written
many years ago.

Now, Keiki . . .
here is a
happy Hapa-Hawaiian
version of
"'Twas the Night
before Christmas"!

’Twas the night before KALĪKIMAKA,

KALĪKIMAKA — CHRISTMAS

When all through the HALE

Not a creature was stirring,

Not even an ‘IOLE;

The KĀKINI were hung
by the PUKA UAHI with care,
In hopes that KANAKALOKA
soon would be there.

KĀKINI — STOCKINGS • PUKA UAHI — CHIMNEY • KANAKALOKA — ST. NICHOLAS; SANTA CLAUS

The KEIKI were nestled all snug in KŌKŌ beds,

KEIKI — CHILDREN • KŌKŌ — STRING HAMMOCK

While visions of KANAKĒ danced in their heads;

KANAKĒ — CANDY

And mama
in her HAINAKĀ LEI,
and I in my PĀPALE cap,
Had just settled down
for a long island nap;

HAINAKĀ LEI — NECKERCHIEF • PĀPALE — HAT, HEAD COVERING

When out on the lawn
there arose such a KULINA,
I sprang from my HIKIE'E
to see what was the PILIKIA.

KULINA — CLATTER • HIKIE'E — LARGE HAWAIIAN COUCH-BED • PILIKIA — TROUBLE, NUISANCE, MATTER

Away to the window
I flew in a WIKIWIKI flash,
Tore open the shutters
and threw up the sash.

WIKIWIKI — FAST, QUICK

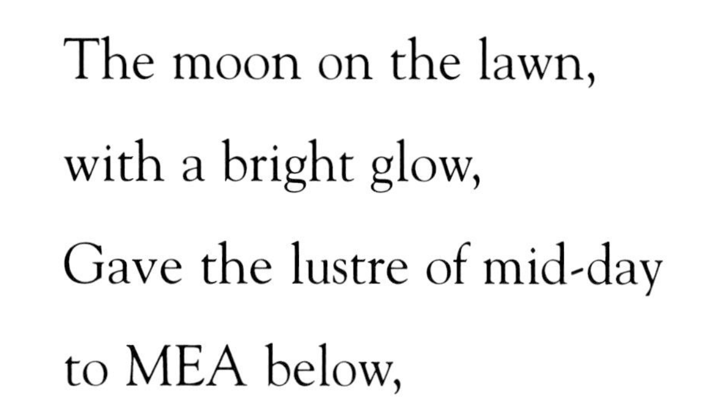

The moon on the lawn,
with a bright glow,
Gave the lustre of mid-day
to MEA below,

When,
what to my wondering MAKA
should appear,
But a MENEHUNE-size sleigh,
and eight LIʻI reindeer,

MAKA — EYES
MENEHUNE — ELF
LIʻI — TINY

With a little old KĀNE,
so lively and quick,
I knew WIKIWIKI it must be
KANAKALOKA—jolly St. Nick.

KĀNE — MAN • WIKIWIKI — FAST, QUICK
KANAKALOKA — ST. NICHOLAS, SANTA CLAUS

More rapid than eagles his KŪKINI they came,

and he whistled, and shouted, and called them by name;

"Now, Dasher! Now, Dancer! Now, Prancer and Vixen!

On, Comet! On, Cupid! On Donder and Blitzen!

To the top of the LĀNAI! To the top of the wall!

Now, HOLO away!

HOLO away!

HOLO away, all!"

KŪKINI — COURSERS • LĀNAI — PORCH • HOLO — DASH, RUN

As dry leaves that in a MAKANI PĀHILI fly,
when they meet with an obstacle, mount to the sky;
so up to the KAUPOKU the coursers they flew,
with the sleigh full of toys, and KANAKALOKA, too.

MAKANI PĀHILI — HURRICANE WIND • KAUPOKU — ROOF • KANAKALOKA — ST. NICHOLAS, SANTA CLAUS

And then, in an ‘IMO‘IMO,
I heard on the KAUPOKU
The prancing and pawing
of each little MĀI‘U‘U —

‘IMO‘IMO — TWINKLING • KAUPOKU — ROOF • MĀI‘U‘U — HOOF

As I drew in my PO'O,

and was turning around,

Down the chimney

KANAKALOKA came with a bound.

PO'O — HEAD • KANAKALOKA — ST. NICHOLAS, SANTA CLAUS

Dear
We wish you a Mele Kalikimaka!

He was dressed all in HULUHULU,
from his head to his foot,
And his LOLE were all tarnished
with ashes and soot;

HULUHULU — FUR • LOLE — CLOTHES

A bundle of MEA PĀ‘ANI
he had flung on his back,
And he looked like a KĀLEPA
just opening his pack.

MEA PĀ‘ANI — TOYS

KĀLEPA — PEDLAR

His MAKA – how they twinkled!

His dimples – how MELE!

His cheeks were like LOKE,

His IHU like a cherry!

His droll little WAHA was drawn up like a bow,

And the beard on his ‘AUWAE was as KEA as snow;

MAKA — EYES • MELE — MERRY • LOKE — ROSES
IHU — NOSE • WAHA — MOUTH • ‘AUWAE — CHIN • KEA — WHITE

A short IPU PAKA
he held tight in his NIHO
And the smoke like a LEI
Went 'round his white PO'O;

IPU PAKA — PIPE • NIHO — TEETH • LEI — WREATH • PO'O — HEAD

He had a broad HELEHELENA and his ʻŌPŪ? What a belly!

It shook, when he laughed, like ʻUMEKE PIHA KELE.

He was a chubby MENEHUNE, a right jolly old elf,

And I laughed, when I saw him, in spite of myself;

HELEHELENA — FACE • ʻŌPŪ — TUMMY, STOMACH • ʻUMEKE PIHA KELE — A BOWL FULL OF JELLY • MENEHUNE —ELF

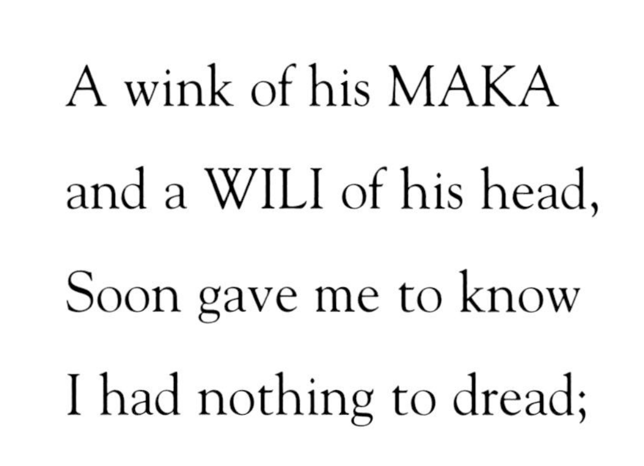

A wink of his MAKA
and a WILI of his head,
Soon gave me to know
I had nothing to dread;

MAKA — EYE • WILI — TWIST

Dear Kanakaloka,
We wish you a Mele Kalikimaka!

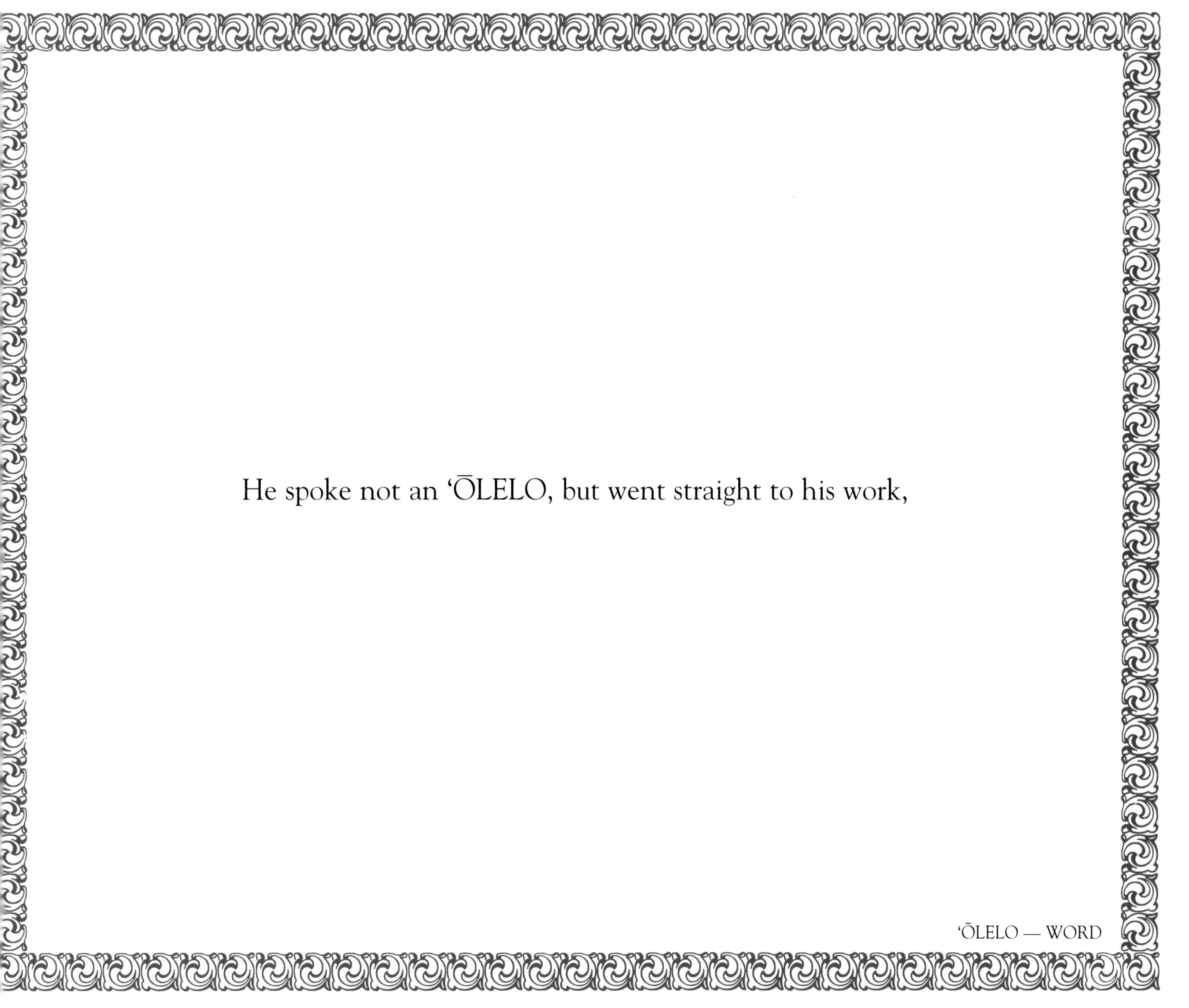

He spoke not an ʻŌLELO, but went straight to his work,

ʻŌLELO — WORD

And filled all the KĀKINI;
then turned with a jerk,

KĀKINI — STOCKINGS

And laying his
MANAMANA KUHI
aside of his nose,
And giving a KŪLOU,
up the PUKA UAHI he rose;

MANAMANA KUHI — INDEX FINGER • KŪLOU — NOD • PUKA UAHI — CHIMNEY

He sprang to his sleigh,
gave his PŪKOLO a whistle,
And away they all flew
like the HEU of a thistle.

PŪKOLO — TEAM • HEU — DOWN

But I heard him HO‘ŌHO,
ere he drove out of sight,

HO‘ŌHO — EXCLAIM

MELE

KALĪKIMAKA to all, and to all

ALOHA!

MELE KALĪKIMAKA — MERRY CHRISTMAS
ALOHA — A FOND FAREWELL, GOOD-BYE

GLOSSARY OF HAWAIIAN WORDS AND PHRASES

Aloha — in this instance, it means a fond farewell, good-bye
'Auwae — chin
Hainakā lei — neckerchief
Hale — house
Helehelena — face
Heu — down
Hikie'e — large Hawaiian couch-bed
Holo — dash, run
Ho'ōho — exclaim
Huluhulu — fur
Ihu — nose
'Imo'imo — twinkling
'Iole — mouse
Ipu paka — pipe
Kākini — stockings
Kālepa — pedlar
Kalīkimaka — Christmas
Kanakaloka — St. Nicholas, Santa Claus
Kanake — candy
Kāne — man
Kaupoku — roof
Kea — white
Keiki — children
Kōkō — string hammock
Kūkini — coursers
Kulina — clatter
Kūlou — nod
Lānai — porch
Lei — wreath
Li'i — tiny
Loke — roses
Lole — clothes
Māi'u'u — hoof
Maka — eyes
Makani pāhili — hurricane wind
Manamana kuhi — index finger
Mea — objects
Mea pā'ani — toys
Mele — merry
Mele Kalīkimaka — Christmas
Menehune — elf
Niho — teeth
'Ōlelo — word
'Ōpū — tummy, stomach
Pāpale — hat, head covering
Pilikia — trouble, nuisance, matter
Po'o — head
Puka uahi — chimney
Pūkolo — team
'Umeke piha kele — a bowl full of jelly
Waha — mouth
Wikiwiki — fast, quick
Wili — twist

Ke ahiahi mamua o Kalīkimaka — The night before Christmas

MELE KALIKIMAKA
Words and Music by
R. ALEX. ANDERSON
Brightly (not too slowly)
mp
Jin — gle Bells up-on a steel gui — tar
Through the palms we see the same bright star
Chorus
mf
Me — le Ka — li — ki — ma — ka is the thing to say On a
bright Ha — wai — ian Christ — mas day
That's the is — land greet — ing that we send to you From the
land where palm trees sway
Here we know that Christ — mas will be green and bright The
sun to shine by day and all the stars that night
Me — le Ka — li — ki — ma — ka is Ha — wa — ii's way to
say Mer — ry Christ — mas to you
1
2
you
(c) Copyright 1949, 1950 by MCA MUSIC, A Division of MCA, INC., New York, N. Y. Sole Selling Agent MCA MUSIC, A Division of MCA, Inc., 445 Park Ave., New York, N. Y. 10022. Used by Permission. All Rights Reserved.